THE SILENT DECEPTION

James Mitchum Oates

Author's Tranquility Press
MARIETTA, GEORGIA

Copyright © 2021 by James Mitchum Oates.

All rights reserved. No part of this publication may be reproduced, distributed or transmitted in any form or by any means, including photocopying, recording, or other electronic or mechanical methods, without the prior written permission of the publisher, except in the case of brief quotations embodied in critical reviews and certain other noncommercial uses permitted by copyright law. For permission requests, write to the publisher, addressed "Attention: Permissions Coordinator," at the address below.

James Mitchum Oates/Author's Tranquility Press
2706 Station Club Drive SW
Marietta, Ga 30060
www.authorstranquilitypress.com

Publisher's Note: This is a work of fiction. Names, characters, places, and incidents are a product of the author's imagination. Locales and public names are sometimes used for atmospheric purposes. Any resemblance to actual people, living or dead, or to businesses, companies, events, institutions, or locales is completely coincidental.

Ordering Information:
Quantity sales. Special discounts are available on quantity purchases by corporations, associations, and others. For details, contact the "Special Sales Department" at the address above.

Silent Deception/James Mitchum Oates
Paperback: 978-1-956480-39-9
eBook: 978-1-956480-40-5

Deceivers are horrible people who lack great moral scrutiny. The worst kinds of deceptions are those done in the dark – or in silence.

CHAPTER ONE

Here I come. One more push oughta get it. Oh my! I see the light. And here I am finally. I didn't feel like crying, but somehow, I sensed that that was the most natural thing to do. Kind-of like if I didn't cry, they would all think something was wrong with me. So, I let it go. I cried and cried and screamed right there in the doctor's arms. Then he handed me to the lady on the bed – the person I came from. There in her arms, I felt secure and safe but continued to cry. She held me and soothed me until finally I fell asleep.

When I finally awakened, I was in a different place. It was dark and secluded and it made me uncomfortable. So,

I began to cry – loud. Then not far from where I was at, I heard a voice say, "I got it." The next thing I knew, someone was lifting me up and rocking me gently. Then he was trying to put something in his hand into my mouth. I received it and began to suck on it and a good-tasting liquid came out. Then I stopped crying.

"He was just hungry," the man then said to the woman lying in bed. This was the same lady who held me in her arms at the other place – the same lady I came from. He then slowly lowered me back into the same dark place and there I slept, being satisfied from having gotten something on my stomach.

Here I was Joshua Eugene McClure. Born March 17, 1991 in Boston, Massachusetts. My mom's name was Clarice Rose McClure. My father's name was Jacob Orville McClure. I have two older brothers. The oldest is Marcus Emmit McClure. The middle brother is not much older than me – not much at all. In fact, only fifteen minutes difference. Yep, he is my twin brother who came out fifteen minutes before me. Right now, he is in his own crib on the other side of the room resting peacefully. His name is Joseph Bernard McClure.

This is my family. This is the way life starts out. As I layed there, I began to dream. The dream was actually a memory.

What can I remember? I was just born.

But as I lay there, the memory hit me hard.

After I came out of the lady, and once the doctor placed me in her arms, she held me and looked in my face and said, "Oh, this one doesn't have dimples like the other one. And even though it is his twin, he is not as cute as his brother. I can see already, this one is probably going to be a problem child."

CHAPTER TWO

At that time, I didn't understand what she said nor did I know what she meant.

Then why was it stuck in my memory?

It was as if it were something I needed to remember, but I didn't know why.

As time went on, the more the memory became more of a blur and the older I got, the more I learned. In fact, I was learning so well, by the time I was in third grade, I was reading books like "Tom Sawyer" and "Huckleberry Finn" courtesy of my teachers. They would very often give me books like these to take home and read. My teachers realized I was very intelligent and that my intelligence level exceeded that of my peers. So one day, they decided to give me an intelligence aptitude test. And just as they predicted, I scored in the high-level ranking above average. The next step was to sit down with my parents and talk about higher level education for me.

One day my mom came to pick up me and Joseph from school as usual. This is when the teachers approached my mom and asked to speak to her in private. They all walked away out of hearing distance leaving me there. I tried and tried to hear what they were saying, but to no avail. But I was very excited. I was excited because I knew what they were talking about. They were discussing me and my intelligence and a possible of me moving up in grades. I began to think and envision myself moving up in grades and being with kids on my level. I thought about the future and where my intelligence could take me. The possibilities were limitless. I thought and envisioned so much that I drifted off and became engrossed in my thought. I finally came to when I saw them coming towards me and I heard one of the teachers reply, "You're making a terrible mistake, Mrs. McClure. An intelligence like his should not be overlooked."

"Look, this is my son," my mom snapped. "I just don't think it's fair. What about Joseph? He's very intelligent too."

"Yes, no one is saying he isn't. But Joshua has a gift. His mind is exceptional. He needs to be around peers of his own intelligence. To deny him of this would be like a crime. I'm just asking you to give it some thought."

"And I'm telling you now, the answer is no. I know what's best for my son. And also, I'll be transferring my sons to new schools as soon as possible."

"But Mrs. McClure..."

"Thank you very much and have a good day."

With that, my mom grabbed my hand and we marched out of there. Never to look back.

My mom and dad argue a lot. Most of the time, I don't know what it's about. But tonight, I knew exactly what it was about.

It was about me.

"You did what!?" I could hear my dad yell.

Then I heard my mom's muffled voice say something, but I couldn't understand what.

"You do realize that was a pretty decent school? It was free for Christ's sake and not only that, but it had pretty quality education. Why the hell would you take them out of there?"

"Do you want to know the real reason why?" mom shouted.

"Yes, it would be fucking great if you would tell me the real reason why."

Suddenly mom's voice became very low and whisper-like – almost as if she knew we were listening but didn't want us to hear.

Finally, after a few minutes of the low mumbling, the door opened and dad came out. I looked at his face, but I couldn't tell what he was thinking because of his expression. It was a very shocking unrecognizable look I had never seen before. But one emotion that I could detect very easily from his expression was sadness.

He then looked at mom and said, "I'll get my stuff in the morning."

He then walked to the doorway and stopped and turned back to mom and replied, "You're going to burn in hell. May God have mercy on your soul."

He then looked at me and put his hand on my shoulder and said, "Take care of yourself." Then he threw a cold stare at mom and while still talking to me, he said, "And be careful." With that, daddy was gone.

CHAPTER THREE

"Mom, is daddy coming back?" Marcus asked as he, Joseph, and I stood in front of the living room window watching the U-Haul tow away the last of his stuff.

It was Saturday morning. Mom was watching T.V.

"No, he's not coming back."

"Why did he leave?" I pleadingly asked.

She then stopped watching T.V. and turned to look at us.

"Come over here a second guys."

The three of us walked over to her and stood around her.

"Listen fellas, you know your father and I loved each other very much like all married couples. But like all married couples we had our problems so we tend to fight a lot. Well, your father and I decided that you guys shouldn't see us fight so much so he thought it best if he left."

"I miss him already," Joseph sobbingly said.

Then Marcus and I began sniffling too.

"Hey, hey guys. Come on. You guys are going to be strong for me, right?" You're my little soldiers. That means no crying. Help me out as much as you can. Things will get better. You'll see. Now, who wants some eggs and toast and orange juice?"

"Oooh me, me..." the three of us said with delight.

"Alright, wait right here and watch T.V. and I'll call you when it's done."

Marcus and Joseph sat on the sofa. I sat on the floor.

We were looking at an episode of "Archie Bunker" when Marcus finally said, "Enough of this. I want to watch cartoons."

But then I replied, "No, I want to see Sesame Street."

I really did want very badly to see "Sesame Street" because I just loved Oscar the Grouch.

"No, I want to see cartoons," Marcus demanded as he picked up the remote.

Joseph was impartial and didn't care one way or the other what was on the screen.

I didn't argue and Marcus began flicking through the channels until he found a cartoon.

We all watched and laughed at "Tom and Jerry."

Then mom called us for breakfast.

When mom cooked like this, it was a special treat.

So we ate and indulged in our eggs, toast, and orange juice. When we were done, we gave our dishes to mom and she washed and put them up. Then we went to our rooms to get dressed.

Marcus had his own room and Joseph and I shared a room. We had separate beds – one on one side of the room and the other one on the other side.

While we were getting dressed, mom came up to me and Joseph's bedroom door and said, "Boys, don't forget what I told you and when you're done, you can go out and play."

After we were dressed, I did what mom asked and Joseph, Marcus, and I went outside with a red ball.

We were playing kickball for about ten minutes when mom called my name from the window.

I came walking towards the house and she met me at the back door.

"Joshua, didn't I tell you to clean your room before going out to play?"

"Yes ma'am, and I did."

"No, you did not. Part of the room is still a mess."

"That's Joseph's side. He said he wasn't going to clean it because you could do it for him."

"No excuses. I told you to clean the room and you lied and said you did."

"I did, but Joseph..."

"No buts. Get in there and clean the entire room and no T.V. or playing outside for a few days should teach you about lying."

"But..."

And back-talking will only make it longer. Do you understand?"

"Yes ma'am."

As I went in, mom said, "Marcus and Joseph, you two can stay out and play as long as you like."

I then went to my room and began cleaning up Joseph's side.

I was puzzled and angry, but more-so hurt.

CHAPTER FOUR

After putting the last pair of shoes in the closet, I slumped into the old wooden chair that sat up against the wall near my dresser. Finally, I was done cleaning this entire room. As I sat there, I heard Marcus and Joseph outside having fun.

That's where I should be.

It was nice and warm today and I felt like playing – not being cooped up in here cleaning up Joseph's mess.

I peeked out the window and saw Marcus running and chasing a frisbee that Joseph sent him.

It wasn't fair. Why was Joseph getting treated the way he was and I was getting treated like crap?

Then it hit me.

Mom must be playing favorites.

But immediately after I got this notion, I hurriedly dismissed it.

"Mom loves us all the same," I thought to myself. "If she didn't, she wouldn't take care of you, give you a place to stay, put clothes on your back and food in your mouth."

Then I thought, "Maybe she's right. I probably should've cleaned the entire room in the first place."

"Well at least it's clean now," I said in a whisper underneath my breath as I rose from the chair and made my way to my bed.

I was exhausted.

Although I wasn't exhausted from cleaning the room; I was exhausted from worry and thought.

I climbed in my bed and got underneath my covers. I closed my eyes and began to think. I thought of my family, including daddy, and just envisioning our family moments and events we've had.

Seconds later I was sleep.

I drifted off to the amusement park we all went to last year. It was exactly like I remembered. Marcus, Joseph, and I were all excited about this trip. It was our first time going to an amusement park. Mom made each one of us a peanut butter and jelly sandwich and dad bought us each a Payday candy bar with a carton of chocolate milk to snack on while we drove there. When we got there, we decided to ride the rides. Mom and dad stood there talking for a moment, then decided that we could split up, but meet back where we were at. Mom then said, "Marcus, Joseph, come on with me."

Dad then looked at me and smiled and said, "That leaves us buddy."

With that, mom, Marcus, and Joseph went their way and dad and I went ours.

We searched for a ride.

Finally, we came up on one called "The Dragonfly."

Then I began, "Ooh, ooh dad, this one, this one!"

I wasn't attracted to the physical structure of "The Dragonfly," nor did it look to be as fun as the others.

I was simply drawn to it because of its name.

Dad paid for our tickets and we were on our way to riding "The Dragonfly."

We got on, got seated and strapped in. A few seconds later it began to move. As the contraption slowly rose to the air, I looked down to see if I could see my mom or brothers. Then we were high in the air. Suddenly we dropped and went side to side as we curved on the tracks and came back up. The people were screaming so loud, I thought I would go deaf before finally realizing that one of the screamers was daddy.

We went up, down, side to side, and around and around before the ride finally slowed to a halt. We got out and my knees were a little wobbly. We then began to walk back to where we said we'd meet the others.

When we got there, they were there waiting.

Dad then said to mom, "Well what'd you guys ride?"

"Oh, something called 'The Centipede.' It wasn't that fun. Joseph threw up. What about you guys?"

I then very excitedly said, "Oh, it was awesome!" We rode this ride called "The Dragonfly." First, we started real high up in the air. Then…"

Then Joseph interrupted, "Are you saying your ride was better than mine?"

"Well, no," I said, "but…"

"But nothing," Joseph interjected, then lunged off and hit me in the ear.

I wasn't going to take that, so I bald my fists up for a challenge.

This is when mom said, "Alright Joshua, that's enough! Stop it right there. What have I told you about fighting?"

This is when daddy stepped up and said, "What the hell's wrong with you? You're directing this at Joshua when Joseph clearly started the fight."

She then replied, "No, I'm not. I just don't want them fighting. Now can we please just find another ride to ride?"

Dad then said, "Alright, but first Joseph has to apologize since he started it."

Mom then said to Joseph, "You heard your father."

Joseph muttled out a very weak, "I'm sorry."

"Now can we please find another ride?" mom said.

Dad then said, "Yes, I saw a few over this way," as he led the way.

Me, mom, Joseph, and Marcus walked behind dad. Then mom grabbed my arm where dad couldn't see and whispered to me, "Next time you won't be so lucky." Then she let me go.

The rest of the trip I was silent and saddened.

Then I woke up.

I smelled spaghetti and garlic toast.

And I was hungry.

As I got up to go eat dinner, I tried to dismiss the dream even though it really happened.

I told myself, "See there you go again making a big deal out of nothing when really we're just one happy family."

I got to the kitchen and saw no one there. The lights were off and there was my plate of spaghetti with garlic toast sitting at my spot at the table.

"What the hell's goin' on here!" I wanted to yell.

Why hadn't anyone awakened me for dinner so I could eat when everyone else did? And why had they turned the light off and just left my food sitting there?

Then I thought back to what I'd just been thinking about on the way to the kitchen.

Was our family happy?

Then I put all of the thoughts together of the amusement park, mom's reaction towards me with the teachers and me going to a higher grade, and what happened with cleaning Joseph's side of the room today. Then quickly that notion of a happy family began to feel like an illusion – with a much more sinister reality.

CHAPTER FIVE

Time passed and as I got older, the more my feelings of love and trust for my family got replaced with doubt and skepticism, but more importantly – fear.

What were they capable of?

Would they ever try to harm me?

Fifth grade was an experience all of its own. I interacted with all kinds of kids and was constantly impressing my teachers with my sharp intelligence.

Then after school one day, I was standing in the courtyard waiting on Marcus and Joseph as usual so we could go home. Suddenly three boys walked up to me. Then without a word, one of them grabbed me and locked my arms up from behind. They were fast, but I was faster.

When one of them came in for a swing, I used my strength to turn my back to him so that he hit the boy holding me. Then the other one charged me and I side-stepped him and stuck my foot out and tripped him. With the other two on the ground, that left me and the last one. He came at me and swung with a right hook. I blocked it, and with my other hand, used my backpack to upper-cut him right in the nose. He fell down screaming and holding his hands to his nose. I could see the blood gushing from in between his fingers. And then the one that got hit by the other one was up. He charged me and when he got to me, he ran right into a knee to the groin. It sent him down immediately and finally the one that I had tripped was up. He very coldly said, "You're in for it now." I then replied, "Let's do this." He then got close enough to me where I could reach him. I grabbed his arm and swung him around and used my hip to flip him to the ground. I had Kung-Fu theatre to thank for that move.

There they lay. All three of them. But it was weird because I didn't know these boys nor had I ever seen them before.

Suddenly Marcus and Joseph came running up and when they got to me, they stopped to look at the carnage.

Marcus then very excitedly asked, "What the hell happened?"

"These guys just attacked me for no reason," I said breathing hard for air.

"Then what?" Joseph asked.

"This..." I replied gesturing my hand to the fallen three.

"Oh my God..." Marcus said looking at Joseph.

"Tell us about it on the way home," Joseph said putting his arm around my shoulder as we began to walk home.

"Mom is going to be so pleased," Joseph said as we arrived to the door. My shoe was untied, so I bent down to tie it. The door was unlocked, so Joseph turned the knob and went in. Marcus followed.

Then I heard mom say, "Did it happen?"

This is when I walked in and asked mom, "Did what happen?"

She looked at me like she was surprised to see me and replied, "Oh I just wanted to know if Joseph spoke to the principal about something."

The whole time she said this, her eyes kept looking away – purposely missing me.

Then Joseph piped up, "Mom, you won't believe what happened at school today. Three boys attacked Joshua and he single-handedly beat them up."

"Well where were you two?" she asked.

"I was in the bathroom," Marcus replied.

"And I was talking to the principal like you asked," Joseph responded.

"Oh honey, are you O.K.?" mom concernedly asked.

"Is he O.K.?" You should ask those boys if they're O.K.," Joseph exclaimed. "Look at him... Not a scratch on him."

"Tell me all about it over a nice big bowl of Rocky Road ice-cream," mom said to me.

We went to the kitchen and as she dished up my ice-cream, I told her the story. I was still talking as I ate. And as I talked and ate, she listened – but her eyes were hiding something.

When I was done talking, she asked, "Would you recognize the boys if you saw them again?"

"Yeah," I said.

"Good, then tomorrow we'll go up there and you point them out and I'll be sure the principal expels them immediately."

"Marcus, Joseph, you two come in here," she called out. "I don't want what happened today to ever happen again. I want you with each other as much as possible. Joshua could've gotten hurt. Do you understand?"

"Yes ma'am," they simultaneously replied.

"Good. Now my little warrior, tonight we're going to celebrate your excellent skill and bravery at Applebee's tonight for dinner. What do you think of that?"

"Wow, thanks mom. You're the greatest," I said giving her a big hug.

That night, we went to Applebee's and it was then and there I gained a new outlook on my family – a positive one.

CHAPTER SIX

After that fight, I hadn't had any altercations with anyone for a while – not even my brothers. Whereas it's normal for brothers to argue and fight every now and then, this was not the case. We all got along very well. Then I entered sixth grade.

I was always very shy so I tended to stay to myself. But thanks to a little encouragement from Joseph, who told me to just try and blend in, I had it a little easier this year. Also, I had more friends. Marcus never had a problem blending in and was always popular. He was growing up to be a fine young man and it seemed like he was getting more and more handsome every day.

Sixth grade work was on a different level than the other grades. But what seemed easy to me seemed to come as a challenge to Joseph. I had no problem understanding and completing my assignments. And I always was scoring at the top of my class. Very often did I find myself helping Joseph with his work.

Then one day before lunch, my teacher took me to the side and handed me a big volume-sized book by Edgar Allan Poe and told me to read it. She said for me to take my time and when I was done to give her a written report with my analysis on the book. I said O.K. and put the book in my backpack. Then I went to lunch. After lunch I headed back upstairs to class and took my seat. Every so often, I noticed my teacher would be just looking at me and smiling. Then the bell rang to go home. Joseph and I found Marcus and we left. That night, I started reading and kept reading until I fell asleep.

A week later, I handed in the report. It was right before lunch.

"Thank you, Joshua," Mrs. Olin said. "I'll start reading this immediately."

"So why did you have me do this report but no one else?" I inquired.

"Well Joshua, I've been monitoring your work for some time now and I have reason to believe that you are of a very high level of intelligence and I think this report is going to confirm that."

"Really?" I excitedly asked.

"Yep, and if it's true, I want to look at getting you to maybe skip a grade or two."

I then looked down.

"Joshua, what's the matter with that? I thought you'd be excited."

"Well, that sounds good and all, but it's just that I had a chance in third grade to skip more grades, but my mom said no. I don't think she'll want that."

"Well, I don't see why not. Tell her to call me or to drop by sometime so we can talk about it."

"O.K."

"Now go on and go to lunch. In the meantime, I'll be reading this."

After lunch, I was headed back to class when I saw Mrs. Olin standing at the door as if she was waiting on me. When I finally reached her, she exclaimed, "It's just as I thought. You are very gifted. I read your report and I must say it was marvelous."

"Thank you," I replied.

"Now I really want to get in contact with your mom about you skipping to higher grades."

"I'll talk to her tonight," I said, then took my seat.

As I sat there, I began thinking of what it would be like to tell mom about what Mrs. Olin said. Before I knew it, it was time to go home.

When I got home, I was very silent. I did my homework, ate dinner, and went to bed. I didn't tell mom.

But I didn't tell her for a reason. I remembered how angry she got at the teachers when I was in third grade. I didn't want that to happen again. Not only that, but I suspect that the night that her and daddy had that big argument, his leaving had something to do with me skipping to higher grades.

So I didn't say a word to mom about what Mrs. Olin said.

The next day in school, I simply told Mrs. Olin that I talked to my mom and she said no and would appreciate it if it were never brought up again. Mrs. Olin said O.K. and that was that.

About a week later, Mrs. Olin gave me a flyer for a poetry contest. I read it and it sparked my interest. The winner would receive $500. So instead of going to lunch that day, I sat in the classroom, with Mrs. Olin's permission, and worked on my masterpiece of a poem. When I was done, I let her read it and she was very excited and confident that my poem could win. I couldn't wait to show mom.

When I got home, I ran in the house and shouted, "Mom, mom, guess what. Great news."

"What is it?" she asked.

I then handed her the flyer for the contest and then handed her my poem.

She glanced over the flyer very quickly. She then began to read my poem. After reading my poem, she said, "Joshua honey, I understand your excitement. But this poem just isn't good enough. But don't worry," she said balding up my poem," I'll help you write something very special next time and I'll make sure you win. O.K. honey?"

"Alright mom."

I was disappointed but more-so hurt because my poem was not good enough. About three weeks had passed and one day my brothers and I were coming home from school.

We were going up the stairs when a strong gust of wind hit us knocking Marcus's papers out of his hand and onto the ground. Joseph helped him pick them up. I went in the house. I heard mom talking and figured she was on the phone. So as not to disturb her, I quietly closed the door. I heard her in her room so that's where I went. I stopped at her door and heard her laughing to someone on the other end. She then said, "Yeah girl, I just went and opened the mailbox and there was that check for $500 for that poem Joshua wrote and I sent in."

CHAPTER SEVEN

I ran to my room and jumped in bed and began to sob in my pillow.

I couldn't believe it.

Mom must've heard me because she came to my room and exclaimed, "Joshua honey, what's wrong?"

"I heard you on the phone just now," I said still sobbing in my pillow. "You told me my poem wasn't good enough. If it wasn't good enough, then why did you turn it in?"

"Joshua, one day you're going to be a great poet or even writer of many books," she said avoiding my question. "But now just isn't the time to focus on such things."

By this time, Marcus and Joseph were in the house. They were standing at the door when mom turned to acknowledge them.

"What's the matter with Joshua?" Marcus asked.

"Oh nothing," mom replied.

"Guys come in here," mom said motioning towards Marcus and Joseph with her hand.

After they stepped into the room, mom then began, "O.K. guys, you know I've been out of work for some time now. But I've got two good pieces of news. First of all, I may have a job at an insurance company. I went to the interview today and I've got a good feeling that I'll get the job. Second, I've met someone. We really like each other a lot."

"So, what's the name of the insurance company?" I asked.

"Global Life Insurance," mom responded.

"So, when do we get to meet this guy?" Joseph asked.

"Actually, he's coming over for dinner tonight, so I want you on your best behavior. I'm cooking a special dinner tonight so go on and get washed up. He'll be here in a few hours."

After I washed very good, I took a nap. When I awakened, I went to the kitchen to see mom, Marcus, and Joseph setting the table for dinner.

Then the doorbell rang.

Mom went to answer it.

She opened the door and replied, "Hi, come on in."

A man with smooth black hair and a nice trimmed mustache and beard stepped in.

But something struck me as odd about him.

Mom then announced, "Paul, this is my youngest son, Joshua," she said motioning to me. "And this is Marcus and Joseph. Boys, say hello to Paul."

We all did and then he replied, "It's a pleasure to meet you all."

"Well Paul, dinner's just about ready. I made Salisbury steak, mashed potatoes, and corn."

"Sounds wonderful," he exclaimed.

"Just sit in here and when dinner's ready, I'll call you."

"Sounds great," he said walking over to sit on the sofa.

Mom, Marcus, and Joseph then went into the kitchen to finish preparing.

I sat in the chair across the couch from Paul.

I had kind of an eerie feeling about him so every now and then, I couldn't help but stare.

Then once he looked up and actually caught me staring.

Before he or I could say anything, mom announced that dinner was ready.

While we ate, I avoided staring at him, figuring it would cause a confrontation.

Mom then piped up, "You know Paul is one of the supervisors at Global Life Insurance."

Why didn't she tell us that the man she is dating works at the company she's going to be working for?

Dinner was excellent!

When we were done, we put our dishes in the sink. Mom said we could worry about washing them later.

We went to our rooms and Paul went to mom's room with her.

I laid on my bed and thought, "Why did I have such an odd feeling about this guy?"

Then I thought about his face and it hit me. I remembered seeing him talking to daddy one time. He was talking to him about life insurance. And from the way they were talking, I could tell they were good friends.

Then I put two and two together. Mom is dating a man that works at a job that she is trying to get on at and he was a good friend of daddy's. Not only that, but he is a supervisor there so he can definitely get her in.

Then it hit me. She is sleeping with one of daddy's friends to get a job.

The nerve of her!

Just the mere thought of her disrespecting daddy like that made my blood boil.

I had to say something.

I hopped out of bed and went and knocked on mom's door.

When she opened it, I stepped in and very sharply asked Paul, "Do you know someone named Jacob McClure?"

He then looked at mom and she looked at him. I could tell they were searching for an answer.

A lie.

"No," he said.

Then I turned around and marched back to my room.

Paul then said to mom, "That one Joshua suspects something." Mom then very coldly replied, "Leave him to me."

CHAPTER EIGHT

When I got back to my room, I wondered where was Joseph.

Oh yeah, he was probably in Marcus's room playing chess.

They do that from time to time.

I only wish they would include me in their fun.

I laid there on my bed wondering what the hell was going on before I finally drifted off.

The next thing I knew, I was in the living room with Marcus and Joseph and mom was in the other room with the door closed talking to someone. Then when I heard the other person speak, I knew it was daddy. Mom then began talking again, but her voice was low and muffled – like she didn't want the three of us to hear what she was saying.

Suddenly daddy opened the door and came out with the saddest most perplexed look I had ever seen. He then told mom he would get his stuff in the morning. Then he walked to the door, and stopped and turned to mom and said, "You're going to burn in hell." He then looked at me and put his hand on my shoulder and said to me, "Take care of yourself. And be careful."

Then he left.

Just the way I remembered.

What could mom have possibly said that was so bad that he would leave his family?

Somehow now, I'm at my mom's bedroom door listening to her on the phone.

"Yeah girl, I just went and opened the mailbox and there was that check for $5oo for that poem Joshua wrote and I sent in."

I ran to my room and jumped in my bed and began to sob in my pillow.

Then mom came to the door and responded, "Go ahead and cry. See if I care."

This isn't how it happened.

Or maybe this is how she was really feeling.

"Yes, I got $500 off of your poem. But that doesn't mean it was as great as you might think. You know you couldn't write a better poem than Marcus or Joseph on your best day. You'll never be as good as either one of them."

Then I woke up.

I was in a cold sweat and breathing hard.

I looked over and saw Joseph laying there sleeping – it was night time.

Then I looked over to my right on my drawer. The clock said 2:37 a.m.

But something was odd. Something was so out of place, I could taste it.

But I hadn't had a clue of what it was.

First of all, I remember when leaving mom and Paul in the room and coming to my room, I laid on the bed.

But I don't remember going to sleep. My mind was a blank about anything or remembering anything after laying down. Then I started to sit up and when I did, I felt a lot of pain.

So much so I wanted to cry out. But I didn't because I didn't want to wake Joseph.

Finally, after a little struggle and taking the pain, I was up. I stood up to go turn the lights on and when I did, I saw the room was a mess – a complete mess.

That's odd because the room didn't look like this before I layed down.

As I stood there thinking, something caught my eye. I looked over at the foot of my bed and saw what looked like the cap to a needle.

I said to myself, "That's crazy, no one here uses needles."

Then I walked over to my bed and picked it up and that's exactly what it was - a cap to a needle. But there was no actual needle or syringe anywhere in sight.

Then I thought and put two and two together. I layed down but don't remember going to sleep. Then when I do wake up, I was sleep for a while and to me it only seemed like a very short time. Not only that, but when I awaken, I am extremely sore. The room is a mess as if there was some kind of a scuffle. And then I find this needle cap but no needle.

So this is what it's come to.

CHAPTER NINE

After that event, I watched my front, back, right, and left at all times – literally. I didn't have any proof of what I think happened had actually happened, but it was enough. Being on constant vigil and watch of my family because of fear of them put me in a state of depression. The years went on and as they did, so did the harboring suspicions of my family. These suspicions carried me through my high school years and finally when I became a senior, I reflected on the entire situation.

One day I stood in front of the mirror and asked myself, "What the hell is going on with you? O.K. so one night many years ago, it may have seemed as if your family drugged you and put you to sleep. But what proof do you have? Also why would they even do something like that? The whole thing sounds ridiculous. It's just an example of my own foolish paranoia. Your family loves you very much and you're very fortunate to have them."

With that, I headed downstairs to eat breakfast and then I was off to school. When I got to school and got to my locker, there she was waiting on me; the love of my life, Nicole Harbert. This was the girl I had been dating since last year. We had grown very close and fond of each other.

"Hey babe."

"Hey Josh. Are we still on for tonight?"

"Yeah, and remember what I told you. Just relax and be yourself. My mom's going to love you."

"Alright I'll be there at 7:00p.m."

"Alright see ya."

"Bye."

"Bye."

With that, we went to our classes. The whole time I thought to myself about how it's going to be tonight. I had butterflies in my stomach. I told her to relax, maybe I should follow the same advice.

Then I thought to myself, "There's nothing to worry about. Mom accepted Marcus's girlfriend and gave them her blessing to move in together when she met her. Then just one month and a half ago, Joseph came home with his girlfriend and announced that they would be getting their own place together when he graduates in May. Yeah, everything should work out fine."

The time flew by so fast, before I knew it, it was time to go home.

When I got home, I went straight to my room to prepare – mentally. The old negative thoughts started to resurface.

What if mom doesn't like her?

What if Nicole doesn't like mom?

Will mom really give me her blessing to move in with this girl when I graduate?

If she does grant us her blessing, will she at least help us until we can get stable and on our feet?

How will Nicole and I survive? We both have to find jobs.

Also I plan on going to college. How are we going to afford that financially?

All of these questions swamped me all at one time. But just as sure as they began to cloud my mind was as fast as I was able to dismiss all of these negative options with one statement, "Leave it in the hands of God."

I then got up and went to the kitchen where mom and Joseph were.

"Hey mom, hey Joseph," I said greeting them as I saw them sitting at the table.

"Hey honey," mom replied looking up at me. She looked tired.

"Mom," I began, "I was thinking. Why don't we have a special dinner tonight?"

"For what reason, honey?"

"Well it's been a long time since we've had a little fried fish and macaroni cheese for dinner."

"Mmm, that sounds delicious," Joseph replied with his eyes closed. He looked as if he were already savoring the meal.

"I don't see why not," mom responded. "I'll get started on it in about an hour."

"And I'll help," Joseph replied.

"Alright, I'll go wash up and change clothes for dinner," I said turning to go to the bathroom.

Once I washed up, I stood in the mirror and looked at myself. Then I said, "Now here comes the best part." And with that, I splashed on the Aqua Velva. Then I got dressed.

When I came out of the bathroom, the savory aroma of fried fish hit me.

Oh, it smelled good!

Then I went to my room and waited.

I was laying on my bed for about forty-five minutes when the bell rang. I looked at the clock. Five minutes early.

Perfect timing.

Then the butterflies began jumping around in my stomach.

"Just calm down, it's going to be fine," I told myself.

With that, I went to introduce Nicole.

When I went to the living room, mom, Joseph, and Nicole were standing there.

"Joshua, this girl says she knows you," mom said looking confused.

"Yes mom, Joseph, this is Nicole, my girlfriend. Nicole, this is my mom and my brother, Joseph."

They both stared at her for a few seconds as if they were looking at a ghost.

"Joshua, I didn't know you had a girlfriend," mom said in dismay.

"I invited her over for dinner so you could meet her," I heartily said. "Kind-of like a surprise."

"Well, we're definitely surprised," Joseph retorted. I could detect the sarcasm in his voice.

"Oh, I'm sorry," mom said snapping out of her daze. "Where are my manners? Right this way," she replied leading her to the kitchen.

I followed.

When we got to the kitchen, mom said, "Joseph, set an extra plate at the table."

As he did that, I could see Nicole taking in the aroma of the fried fish.

"The dinner smells wonderful, Mrs. McClure," Nicole responded.

"Please call me Clarice."

Before long, the table was set and we all sat down to dinner.

"So tell me dear, how did you and Joshua meet?"

"Well, last year we had a class together that was right before lunch. And one day, class let out and we went to lunch, but when we got to the cafeteria, there was only one table that was vacant. So we sat at that table together. It was then and there we talked and I liked him and he liked me so we decided to sit together at lunch every day. Then we decided to become boyfriend and girlfriend."

"Interesting," Joseph replied.

Once again, I could detect the sarcasm in his voice.

"Yeah, we really like each other. So much so, we were hoping to move in together when we graduate in May," I announced.

Joseph began coughing.

"Joshua, that's a really big step," mom exclaimed.

"But you gave Joseph your blessing for the exact same thing."

What mom said next shocked me. She replied, "You're right. Alright honey, you have my blessing."

"Oh, thanks mom, you're the greatest."

I looked at Joseph who looked perplexed.

The rest of the dinner we ate in silence.

When we were done, I walked Nicole to the door. Mom and Joseph were still in the kitchen.

"Mom, what's going on? You're really going to let him go like that?"

"Now Joseph, you know me better than that."

CHAPTER TEN

Here it is. The big day.

I'm so nervous.

There I stood side by side with Joseph at the altar, both of us looking ever-so nice in our suits. Then I saw her at the end of the aisle. She was breathtaking. It was like looking at an angel. My bride to be, Nicole Harbert.

The church lights were somewhat dim, but I could see her face just as clearly and plain as ever. The place was packed with lots of attendants. Then she began her voyage to the altar where we would consummate our love for one another. With every single step she took, the butterflies built up in my stomach more and more. By the time she reached the altar, my stomach was hurting and I wasn't sure if this was what I really wanted to do.

But it's too late to turn back now.

I went and took my place next to her and the preacher began. As he talked, my mind began to wander. It wandered back to the first time I met her and how I felt when I saw her. It was then and there I believed in love at first sight.

Then I heard, "The ring please." I was still in a sort-of trans until the pastor cleared his throat and said, "Joshua, the ring please."

I snapped out of it. "Oh yes, here it is," I said digging in my pocket. As I held the ring in my hand about to put it on her finger, I recited my vows to my bride to be. Then I put it on her finger. She then got out her ring and recited her vows to me and then placed the ring on my finger.

Then the pastor replied, "If there is anyone here now who sees why this couple should not be married, let them speak now or forever hold their peace."

Then I heard a voice say, "I don't think they should be married."

I looked to my right at the first pew.

It was mom.

My eyes got wide.

The pastor then asked her, "On what grounds?"

Then mom's mouth turned up into a sneer and she replied, "On the grounds of..."

Then I hopped up.

I was sweating. Not because of the heat in my room because it wasn't hot. But because of fear.

Would my own mother really try and sabotage my wedding?

Why mom? On what grounds do you think I shouldn't get married?

I sat there for a moment pondering the dream. It was a nice day today. The weather was nice and just a perfect day for Thanksgiving. The clock said 4:12p.m. Marcus was coming over tonight for dinner and bringing his girlfriend. I decided to see what I could do to help mom get dinner prepared. I walked into the kitchen to see Joseph putting the icing on a strawberry cake. Mom was at the kitchen sink taking the bones out of the chicken.

"Hi mom. Hey Joseph."

"Hey honey," mom replied looking away from the chicken and up at me.

"Hey Josh," Joseph said still icing the cake with his eyes fixed down.

"I just came to see what I can do to help."

"Well we can certainly use your help because there's plenty to be done," mom replied.

I washed the greens and helped cook the macaroni and cheese and the dressing.

A few hours later, we were done. No sooner than when I went to wash my hands, the bell rang.

I was still washing my hands when I heard Marcus's voice in the living room.

When I walked to the living room, there was Marcus and his girlfriend. He very heartily said, "Hey Josh, how ya doin'?"

"I'm doin' good, Marcus. How are you?"

"Doin' great. You remember Ashley," he said motioning to his girlfriend.

"How are you?" I responded.

"Good," she replied.

"Marcus, you're going to love this dinner," mom excitedly said.

"It smells great," he exclaimed.

Then we all made our way to the kitchen.

When we got to the kitchen and got seated, we all dished our plates up. Then Joseph picked up one of the dinner rolls off of his plate and started to take a bite when he heard mom clear her throat and he looked at her and she was looking at him.

"Did we forget something, Joseph?"

"Oh yeah, he replied folding his hands and bowing his head."

"Josh, would you do the honors?" mom said with her eyes closed and head bowed.

I began:

Gracious Lord, we as a family have so much to be thankful for. You've blessed us with so many things, and now this wonderful meal. Although I do realize that there are many who are less fortunate than we are on this Thanksgiving holiday. I ask that You bless them the way You've blessed us. Comfort them. Show them the love You've shown us in Your divine grace. So we thank You for this great meal and ask for many more like it. For it is in the holy name of Jesus we pray. Amen.

After I said, "Amen," I could hear the others around the table saying, "Amen."

Although I just sat there with my eyes closed for a few seconds longer. I wasn't quite sure why. It was like I was waiting on something.

But what?

Perhaps for something from God to let me know that He heard my prayer.

"Josh, are you O.K.?" I heard mom say.

"Yeah, I'm fine," I said opening my eyes. "I was just doing a little extra praying."

Then I happened to look over at Joseph who was greatly indulging in his food. I then began to eat.

Everyone was silent while we ate. Every now and then there was an occasional, "Can you pass...?"

"Can you pass the ham?"

"Can you pass the greens?"

Then about halfway through the meal, Marcus announced, "Ashley and I are getting married."

The entire room fell silent and all eyes were on Marcus and Ashley. Even Joseph had stopped eating for a minute.

"Well honey, I don't know what to say," mom finally responded.

"Say we have your blessing," Marcus replied.

"But Marcus, marriage is such a big step. Have you planned this out yet? And also you have to have a nice amount of money saved up in case you want to go to college or start a family or..."

"Yes we know," Marcus interrupted, "and we've thought about all of that. But we have the strongest thing anyone can have in any relationship – love. Not only that, but we're happy."

Suddenly mom's worried look went from a frown to a smile. "O.K. honey, if you're happy, that's all that matters.

And I'll help support you financially and help you any way I can. You have my blessing."

Then I thought about the dream I had earlier of my own wedding. I thought about how mom sat in the front row and verbally disapproved of my marriage.

Will I ever get married?

Will I ever be happy?

CHAPTER ELEVEN

"Ho, ho, ho, Merry Christmas," Marcus announced as he came into the living room dressed in his Santa Claus suit. "Josh, have you been naughty or nice?"

We all burst into laughter. This was our Christmas celebration. Everyone was there. It was me, Joseph, and Marcus, all three of our girlfriends, and mom. The only person missing was daddy.

It was odd because I was at the store the other day and I thought I saw a man who resembled daddy very much. I was in the check-out line and he was just leaving. I started to call his name, but then decided just let it go.

Just let it go.

I looked over at Marcus sitting by the tree with his wife. I then recalled the ceremony. I vividly remembered the vows they took to love one another for the rest of their lives, how pretty she was in her dress, and how handsome he was in his nice suit.

As the presents got passed out, I thought of how out of all of the presents I receive and no matter what they are, my biggest and best gift would actually come in May when I get to move in with Nicole.

Then Marcus announced, "To Josh, from mom," while reading the present. He then handed it to me.

I joyfully took it and tore the paper off. Then Nicole asked, "What do you think it is?"

"I don't know, but I'm about to find out," I said finally getting all of the paper off.

It was a box.

I opened it to see a brown sweater. I held it up and looked at it. I said, "Wow, thanks mom," pretending to like it. It was the ugliest thing I had ever seen before in my life.

"Try it on," mom said smiling at me.

So I did.

It was very snug and I couldn't breathe in it. I took it off to look at the size and it was two sizes too small.

Mom then saw the discomfort on my face and replied, "What's the matter, honey? Don't you like it?"

"It's too small," I said.

"Well looks like someone needs to lose some weight," she mockingly retorted.

"Let's see, from mom to Joseph," Marcus said reading another gift.

He then handed Joseph a small wrapped box.

Joseph tore the paper off and opened the box. He pulled out a set of keys. Joseph then replied, "What is this? You give me a set of keys for Christmas. I wanted something good like I always get. What is this for?"

I then began to laugh thinking we both got crappy gifts for Christmas until mom told Joseph to go look outside.

We all did and there it was – a cherry red Lexus.

Joseph literally screamed and said, "Oh my God! Mom, I love you! Can I take her for a spin?"

"You sure can, honey. You and Melanie go on. Have a good time."

Without hesitation, Joseph grabbed Melanie's hand and they were out the door.

This was an extra hard slap in the face. But then it made sense. I remembered mom taking Joseph to get his license a couple of weeks ago. Then when I asked to get mine, she told me to wait until I was sure I was ready to drive.

She planned this all along. I decided not to back down from this one. I then said, "But mom, I wanted to get my license too but you said no."

"Joshua, don't be jealous. Believe me, I have a much bigger and better gift for you and you'll see it next week. Just be patient."

So I was.

Three weeks later passed and still nothing. She didn't say anything else about it and neither did I. Although all the while my suspicions were confirmed – she didn't have such a gift for me in the first place.

But I still had the gift coming up in May of moving in with Nicole. Moving in with Nicole was a great gift because getting away from my immediate family was the best I could ever want.

CHAPTER TWELVE

The big day is here – graduation. Both Joseph and I look so handsome in our suits. Here Joseph and I stood in the mirror getting ready to go to the ceremony we've dreamed of all our lives. Mom was just putting on the finishing touches.

"Here you go, Josh," mom said adjusting my tie. "The tie's a little crooked."

Then she just stared at me and Joseph with a smile on her face. I could see the tears welling up in her eyes.

"Oh my God. My babies have done it. I'm so proud of you."

"Now, now mom," Joseph said walking up to mom and patting her on the back to soothe her. "Don't cry."

"I just can't help it. My boys have become men."

Then Marcus came and peeked around the corner. "Are we ready? We don't want to be late."

"Just give us two more minutes," mom sobbingly said.

Then Marcus was gone.

"Josh honey, come here. You know I love the three of you very much. I don't want anything but the best for you. It's going to be a little tough for you when you move in with your girlfriends at first, but it's going to be even tougher on me. But I'll do everything I can to make sure you have everything you need to live the lives you want."

Marcus peeked his head around the corner again.

"Mom, we have to be there so we know where we're sitting and they're going to start soon."

"Alright guys, you ready?" mom said wiping her eyes.

"Well Josh, this is it," Joseph said putting his hand on my shoulder.

Marcus was still standing there and said, "Aren't we taking my car?"

"I thought we were taking mine," Joseph replied.

"Let's take Joseph's," mom responded. "So he can show it off."

Then I remembered the gift mom promised me, but never came. Suddenly my urge to graduate became stronger.

The graduation was wonderful. After the ceremony, we all went to the Golden Coral restaurant. I've never seen Joseph eat so much in all my life. Two weeks later, Joseph was getting his things packed up to move out. My plans were to start getting packed up a week after Joseph had left because Nicole and I had to work some things out with the apartment we were moving in. The last thing Joseph said to me before he left was, "Take care of yourself."

Then he was gone.

I had most of my stuff packed up the day Nicole and I were at the apartment talking to the landlord. I had only a few things left at the house.

Suddenly my phone rings. I looked at the number. It was Joseph. I very quickly hit the answer button and before Joseph could say anything, I said, "Joe, I'll have to call you back. Right now, me and Nicole are talking to the landlord about getting this place."

Then I hung up.

The phone rang again.

I let it go to voicemail.

Then it rang again and again.

I thought that was odd so I answered.

When I did, I heard Joseph screaming and out of breath, "Josh, you have to come now! Something's wrong with mom!"

"I'm on my way."

Nicole drove fast to get me home.

When I got there, Joseph was sitting on the couch holding mom's hand.

She was lying down.

"Mom, what's wrong?" I exclaimed. She looked terrible.

"Josh, is that you, honey?"

"Yeah mom, it's me," I said taking her other hand.

"One minute I was cleaning the bathroom and the next minute Joseph was standing over me trying to get me conscious. I must have fell out. Not only that, but I can't move my left arm or left leg."

"O.K., I'm calling the hospital," I said pulling out my phone.

"No, no need for all that. I'm sure it's nothing. I went to the doctor a few months ago and he told me I had a few heart problems but nothing serious."

"But how will you get around if you can't move your arm and the other leg."

She then looked at me with pleading eyes and said, "Oh Josh honey, I would hate to ask you to postpone moving in with Nicole. I know how much you wanted to. But only for a few months until I can get my strength up and get strong again."

"O.K. mom."

"Thanks honey, I knew I could count on you."

CHAPTER THIRTEEN

"There you go mom," I said adjusting the pillow for her feet.

"Thank you, honey. Before you leave, did you clean the kitchen?"

"Yep, it's already done. I'm headed out now. I'll see you a little bit later."

"Alright have a good day at work."

With that, I closed the door.

I was headed to work. My first job that is. I had two jobs. I had to in order to support me and mom. She had disability checks coming in for her stroke, but she claimed that wasn't enough. I was a manager at McDonald's and also, I cleaned hotel rooms at the Embassy Suite. All of my dreams of moving in with Nicole and going to college, getting a really good job, and possibly starting a family soon dwindled away. I saw less and less of Nicole. In fact, I saw her so little that the last time we talked, we both decided it would be best if we split up so that I could handle my priorities better.

I felt trapped.

Here I was in good spirits at work today. I was in the office counting money while the other employees were working.

Suddenly when coming out of the office, I saw something that startled me. It was someone in line waiting to place their order. There were two people ahead of him.

It was daddy!

Although seeing him standing there, he had changed so much physically that I had to be sure it was him. I walked over to the employee taking the orders and told her, "I'll take it from here."

He didn't even notice me. But then it was his turn to order and when he looked at me, he looked me directly in the eyes for a few seconds before he cried out, "Joshua? Is that you?"

"Yes, dad it's me."

Then he got misty-eyed and I began to get all choked up. As I came from behind the counter, he met me there with arms wide open. There we stood embraced in a hug. I could feel the stares of the employees and customers. But that didn't bother me. Here I was with my father.

Finally after a while of much sentiment, he replied, "I know that you're in the middle of work now, so I'll give you my phone number so you can call me."

He pulled out a piece of paper and I had an ink pen in my pocket. He wrote his number down and left. At that point, whereas I was already having a good day, just seeing daddy and getting his phone number which let me know that I would be able to keep in contact with him, made my day ten times better.

Along with seeing my father today, I got a new found peace of mind on the way home. I was in the store looking to buy a carton of Rocky Road ice cream when a flyer caught my eye. It read: "Do you have a book or manuscript you would like to publish? If so, then Gallery Books is the company to help get you started."

It then had a phone number listed on the bottom.

But I didn't have a piece of paper, or pen or pencil. Although I was so excited about the thought of me becoming a writer, I decided not to let that stop me. I memorized the phone number and when I got home, I called immediately. I spoke to a representative named Chad who was very helpful. He answered all of my questions and informed me that there would be a $400 fee to publish my book.

$400 I didn't have.

But I was so determined that I started saving.

$20 here and $5 there.

While I saved, I worked on my book. In between working two jobs, taking care of mom, and making sure the house stayed clean, I wrote and wrote. Needless to say, I got very little sleep.

But then finally I got it done. And I had the $400. I sent it in for Gallery Books to publish it. It was a fiction book entitled, "Forbidden Truth." I decided not to let mom know a thing until the book arrives at the house.

She is going to be so surprised!

A week later, the UPS man rang the doorbell and a box was delivered.

Mom was lying on the couch.

"Josh honey, what did the UPS man bring?"

"Alright mom, I've got a surprise for you. Sometime ago, I was in the store and I saw a flyer about publishing a book. I got the number and called and they told me it was a $400 fee. So, I started saving up and as I did, I actually wrote a book. And here it is," I said motioning to the unopened box in my hand.

Mom quickly sat up and replied, "You did what?"

I looked at her in amazement and exclaimed, "Careful mom, your back."

She then began to moan in pain, "Oh my back, my back!"

I walked to the couch she was on, sat down and opened the box.

Here it was.

Forbidden Truth.

I was so enthralled with my book, I didn't notice the look on mom's face until I happened to quickly look up and at her.

Then I saw the glare in her eyes.

This was a look of horrid evil that I had seen from her a few times in my life as a boy growing up.

Then she looked away from me and fixed her eyes on the book and a smile came across her lips.

Then she said, "Josh honey, I'm so proud of you."

CHAPTER FOURTEEN

"Josh, this is great. How'd you do it?" Marcus asked as he, Joseph, mom and I are seated in the living room looking at the manuscript I worked so hard on.

"Honestly, it wasn't that hard. I just sat down and began writing and the thoughts kept coming to me. The only hard part was saving up the money to get it published."

"I always said you were a genius, honey," mom said rubbing my hair.

"Guess what, Josh. I'm going to help you market your book and get it sold so that in no time soon, you'll be raking in money."

"Oh thanks, Joseph. You're the best. You know what I was thinking? I was thinking of maybe looking into enrolling into a college program and possibly getting a degree in creative writing. Who knows, from there I can probably get a license to actually teach English or Creative Writing and do that at a school as a professor."

The three of them looked at each other in bafflement.

"Josh honey, writing a book is great and all, but don't jump way ahead of yourself so fast. You want to start small first. Let Joseph help you market your book first, then look at going to college and possibly becoming a professor."

What she said actually made sense.

But what was her intent in telling me to wait?

I sat there for a minute and looked at them remark on how good the book looked and how nice the summary sounded. I thought to myself about Nicole.

Oh how I missed her.

I decided to call her and see how she was doing and maybe invite her to lunch and show her this wonderful surprise.

Then I stood up and picked my book up off of the table and announced, "O.K., well I have to get going now. The boss doesn't like it when I'm late."

"Alright Josh," Joseph said.

"Josh, you make me so proud to call you my little brother," Marcus replied.

I looked at him. I looked directly in his eyes.

It was like I could see right through him.

I then went upstairs to call Nicole.

I got to my room, sat on my bed, pulled my phone out and dialed Nicole.

"Hello."

"Hey babe."

"Josh...?"

"Yeah, how ya doin'?"

"Oh I'm doin' alright. How 'bout you?"

"Well I'm doin' a lot better now that I hear your voice. Hey listen, I was thinking maybe we could do lunch today."

"Sounds great. What time should I pick you up?"

"Can you meet me on 39th Fairfax in ten minutes?"

"Sure."

"Alright bye."

"Bye."

Then I came downstairs with my book tucked in my front pants and my shirt hanging over it. Then without a word, I left.

Fairfax was actually a block from the street I stayed on and we lived on 37th street. I could've had Nicole pick me up at my house, but somehow, I felt it better if she didn't.

I got to 39th Fairfax and two minutes later, Nicole pulled up.

I got in. We decided on Pickleman's for lunch.

When we got there and walked in, the aroma of fresh pizza hit us. We couldn't have chosen a better place.

And I was hungry. We took seat at a table near the window. The table was wooden with a few smeared spots on the surface and some crumbs on the seat.

But I was so hungry I just sat down and waited for a waiter or waitress to come take our order.

"Nicole, I've got a surprise for you," I said pulling out the copy of "Forbidden Truth" from out of my front pants and handing it to her.

"What's this?" she remarked looking at it and then turning it over to study it.

"I actually wrote that book."

Then a dark-haired gentleman who appeared to be around his early twenty's approached us.

"Hi, my name is Kevin. And what can I get you guys to drink for starters?"

Nicole then responded, "I'll have a Dr. Pepper."

"And you, sir?" Kevin said directing his attention towards me.

"I'll just have a Coke."

"Will Pepsi be O.K.?"

"That's fine."

"Alright here are your menus," he said placing a menu in front of Nicole and one in front of me.

"I'll be right back with your drinks," he replied. Then he turned around and walked away and, in a few steps, he was gone.

"Josh, did you really write this book? How did you do this? This is amazing!" she said glaring at the front cover of the book.

"Well writing the book was easy. The only hard part was saving enough money to get it published."

Then my stomach growled. And Nicole heard it.

"Do you mind if we go ahead and order now?" I embarrassingly asked.

"Not a problem. I totally understand," she replied and then let out a little laugh.

Even though I couldn't see it, I knew I was blushing.

We were both looking through our menus when Nicole replied, "Oh, this looks good."

"What is it?" I asked looking up from my menu at her.

"The chicken fettucine alfredo."

By that time, I had already decided on the angel hair pasta with sautéed mushrooms.

Then Kevin came back.

He set Nicole's Dr. Pepper in front of her with a straw. Then he set my Pepsi in front of me with a straw as well.

"Are you guys ready to order?"

"Yeah," I announced. I'll have the angel hair pasta with sautéed mushrooms."

Kevin began writing this down on his pad. "And you?" he asked Nicole while still writing.

"I'll just have the chicken fettucine alfredo."

"Alright," Kevin said writing Nicole's order down.

When he was done, he picked the menus up and said, "It'll be out shortly," then disappeared in the back again.

Then Nicole had my book in her hands again reading the summary of the book. I could tell that she was impressed with what she was reading. Then when she got to a certain part, she smiled a smile that said she was amused.

But it wasn't just any smile. It was a half-smile that showed her gorgeous dimple. It was this same smile that I came to love so much about her. Although by me being away from her for so long, it was this smile that I came to remember and miss terribly.

I so badly wanted her back.

"Nicole babe, listen," I said reaching my hands across the table to hold hers.

"I still have feelings for you. Now I know we haven't talked about our relationship in a while, but I think it's time we do because I miss you."

"Oh Josh, I miss you too. But do you really think it's going to work out? I mean you having to take care of your mom is a big responsibility and there's just no time for us to really be together or commit to a relationship."

"Well then I'll make time."

"I wish it were that easy, but we have to do what we have to do. Believe me I want to be with you as badly as you want to be with me, but right now that doesn't seem possible."

Then Kevin came walking back to our table with two trays, one in each hand.

"O.K., for you sir, here is the angel hair pasta with sautéed mushrooms," he announced setting my plate in front of me.

"And for you ma'am, the chicken fettucine alfredo," he said as he set Nicole's plate in front of her.

"Is there anything else I can get you?" Kevin asked surveying the table.

"No, thank you," I gratefully replied.

"Alright, enjoy your meal," Kevin responded and then he was gone again.

Here I was with this wonderful meal in front of me. Even though I was very hungry, I hardly noticed it. I couldn't eat because of the fact that I was trying to win Nicole's heart back to me and her response was no.

Was she rejecting me?

"I understand what you're saying, Nicole. But before you make any final decisions, let's think it over. I think we can work it out."

"Maybe we can work it out. O.K., I'll think about it. Now let's eat before our food gets cold."

CHAPTER FIFTEEN

"Oh thank you, honey," mom replied sitting up to take the glass of orange juice that I prepared for her.

"Now this is freshly squeezed?" she inquired.

"Yep, just the way you like."

"So mom, how do you feel about the book I wrote and now I am an actual writer?"

"I think it's wonderful, honey. Oh Josh, did you clean the bathroom yet?" she said trying to quickly change the subject.

"Yes, the bathroom is done. But I'm talking about something way more important than the bathroom."

"Oh honey, I couldn't be more proud of you. I always knew you had it in you. You know when you were born, I remember lying in that hospital bed and holding you in my arms. You were such a tiny sweet thing. And I love you, Joseph, and Marcus all the same, but there was something uniquely different about you from your brothers. When I looked in your eyes, there was this look. It was then that I looked at your father and said, "This one is going to do some great things in his life."

I looked at the way her mouth was twisted a little.

"Speaking of daddy, can we talk about him for a little bit? Tell me what you can."

"Well, I can tell you this – to know your father was to love him. He really was a great man. He cared so much for me and your brothers."

"Well if he cared so much for us, why did he leave?"

"Your father and I had problems in our relationship like any relationship so we decided to split up."

"Something I always wondered about is what happened on the night daddy actually left? I remember you and him were arguing in the other room with the door closed. Then I couldn't hear what either one of you were saying because your voices were really low and muffled. Then when daddy came out of the room, he had the most perplexed horrid look on his face. And then what he said to me before he left. It just didn't make any sense."

"You know, I don't remember. But I know it was something very important."

"But can you try to remember? It's very important for me to know why my father left all of a sudden like that."

"Oh, my neck! There's a sharp pain in my neck. Can you adjust my pillow?"

It was like she was purposely avoiding the question. Then she let out another groan. A very loud groan.

"Oh my God! What's going on? My neck and my back are in terrible terrible pain."

"Do you want me to call a doctor?"

"No," she winced, "just get me some ice packs."

I ran to the kitchen to get the ice packs. When I came back, she was just lying there with a horrid look on her face.

"Here you go, mom," I said rushing to her.

I could see the relief on her face as I put the packs on her back and neck.

"Thank you, honey. Josh, don't you have to be at work in a little bit?"

"Oh yeah, I do," I said looking at my watch. Little did she know I was off today. "I'd better get ready."

But I had other plans. I went upstairs to call Nicole.

I got to my room, sat on my bed, and pulled my phone out, and dialed her number.

"Hello."

"Hey Nicole. It's Josh."

"Oh hey, Josh. What's up?"

"Oh nothing – just wanted to hear your sweet voice. Listen, did you want to get together today?"

"O.K. sure. Where'd you want to go?"

"I was thinking how about just some old-fashioned walking?"

"Sounds good."

"O.K., meet me where we met last time on 39th Fairfax."

"Alright, I'm on my way."

"O.K., see ya in a minute."

"Alright bye."

"Bye."

Then I headed downstairs.

When I got downstairs, mom was lying down sleeping. So as not to wake her, I silently crept to the door, easily opened it so as not to make too much noise, and slowly stepped out.

I quietly closed the door. Then I breathed the fresh crisp air and began to make my way down the street to 39th Fairfax to meet with the love of my life.

I walked and as I did I thought. All I could think of was the night daddy left. I tried to recall what was said and what they were arguing about.

What did she say to you to make you leave your entire family all in one night?

Then I was at 39th Fairfax.

I stood there waiting a good seven to eight minutes when Nicole came pulling up.

As she parked the car, she rolled the window down.

"Hey stranger," she teased. Then she got out, closed the door, and walked up to me.

I gave her a hug while at the same time wanting to give her a kiss on the cheek. But I didn't kiss her; careful not to let my strong emotions show.

But then she surprised me with a kiss on my cheek!

"Josh, I been thinkin' about you and the things you were saying, and I know we can work it out."

"Who are you and what have you done with Nicole?" I joked.

"I'm serious, babe. I was thinking about you all week long," she said while seductively stroking my hand.

I felt a lump in my throat. I didn't want to make any sudden movements for fear that I'd wake up.

Then she looked longingly into my eyes and then kissed me on the lips. The passion from that mere kiss let me know it was very much real.

"Nicole..., uh w-what are you doing?" I stuttered.

"You are trying to make this work, aren't you?"

"Yeah definitely."

"Josh, let's stop playing games. I want you."

"O.K., one second," I said pinching myself to make sure it wasn't a dream.

"What do ya say we go back to my place?"

When I was sure I wasn't dreaming, I said, "Let's go," and we hopped in her car.

CHAPTER SIXTEEN

"Josh, you were amazing."

"You were too, babe. So aside from me being a really great lover, what do you think of me as a writer? I mean have you started reading the book?"

"Actually, I have. I'm on Chapter nine now. It is an extremely good book. I must say in reading this book is one of the reasons I changed my mind so fast about giving you a second chance. Just reading and seeing how creative and intelligent you are is a real turn on. It made me want you so bad."

"In that case read more."

After a while, Nicole and I began to get very close. My feelings for her got very deep and I knew she felt the same.

When I would be at home when all of my chores were done and with nothing to do, I would spend those moments on the phone talking to Nicole.

Could this be love?

Whatever it was, it felt great.

Nicole and I were out getting ice cream one day. We just left Baskin and Robbins.

"You know, this Cherry Blossoms is da bomb," Nicole said taking a bite of her ice cream.

"Yeah, I like how they put a lot of cherries in it," I said taking a bite of my peanut brittle ice cream.

"You know, Nicole, there is something I wanted to talk to you about," I said trying to sound serious.

"What's that?" she inquired not looking at me but still indulging in her ice cream.

"Well, I've been thinking. We've grown very close these past few months and whereas we were going to move in together until my mom got ill, I think we should look at trying to move in together again."

"Josh, I've been thinking the same thing. But you know that seems pretty impossible. Who'll take care of your mom?"

"Well, I've been thinking about having a nurse's aide come to the house and take care of her."

"You've really thought this through, haven't you?"

"Of course, I have. It's only fair that we be together. Not only that, but as far as my writing goes, when I'm with you, I feel inspired. I know that if we're together, I can write lots of great books and we can make good money."

"That sounds great."

"O.K., I'll start packing my stuff up tonight."

Then she turned to me and we both knew what it was time for – a kiss. We both slowly leaned in closer to each other; just like in the movies. The kiss was warm and passionate. I could taste the cherry blossoms on her lips.

When we were done kissing, I pulled back to see my ice cream had fallen out of the cone and onto the ground.

But I didn't care.

I was just so excited and anxious to get home and start packing.

But then the big challenge – how to explain it to mom.

"Well mom, there comes a time in every man's life when he has to make a decision for himself on what he really wants and my decision is I want to leave," I said to myself practicing at the door.

Then I put my key in the door and walked in.

There she was lying on the sofa sleeping. Then I thought to myself, "How can you be so selfish? You know mom is depending on you."

It was right then I decided to avoid telling her anything for as long as possible – even if it came down to the last minute.

I went upstairs and decided to get some rest.

The clock said 9:11 a.m. when I awakened to roll over and look at it. I quickly hopped out of bed and threw my clothes, socks, and shoes on. Then I sprayed on a little bit of Polo cologne and combed my hair.

I was late for work.

I quickly ran downstairs to see mom still sleeping. I woke her up.

"Mom, mom," I called out while nudging her shoulder.

"Oh hey," she responded while turning over to see me.

"Is there anything you need before I leave? I'm late for work."

"Oh, if you would just fix me a bowl of cereal. That should hold me till you get back."

"O.K.," I replied, then quickly walked into the kitchen and dished up a bowl of Sugar Frosted Flakes. Then I took out the orange juice and poured a glass.

When I walked back into the living room she was sitting up.

I set the orange juice and the bowl of cereal on the table. She then picked up the glass of orange juice and asked, "Is this freshly squeezed?"

"No, sorry. I didn't have time."

"Then please take it back. You know I won't drink it unless it's freshly squeezed."

"Sorry," I apologetically replied and picked up the glass and went into the kitchen.

There I stood at the sink and I began to pour. But as I poured the orange juice out, I thought to myself, "That's odd, I've seen her drink orange juice before that wasn't freshly squeezed.

Then I headed to the living room and towards the front door.

"Bye mom. I'll see you soon."

"O.K. honey, I'll see you later."

With that, I was out the door and on my way to work.

Around 10:45 a.m. the doorbell rang.

"Come on in. The door is unlocked," mom announced while lying on the couch.

And in stepped Nicole.

"Hi, Mrs. McClure," she politely said.

"Oh, hi Nicole. How are you?"

"I'm good. I was just wondering is Josh home?"

"No, he's gone to work. I thought you two weren't still talking to one another."

"Oh, Josh and I talk all the time."

"Really? When was the last time you spoke to him?"

"Just yesterday. We went out for ice cream and just talked."

"About what?"

"About all kinds of stuff."

"What kinds of stuff?"

"Oh, I'm sorry. Josh hasn't told you already, then I don't want to intrude. I'll leave it up to him."

"Intrude. Heavens no. Come on and sit here next to me and speak."

"Really I don't know if I should. I think this is something Josh has to do."

"Oh, don't be silly. I'm all ears."

"O.K. Well for some time now Josh and I have been getting more serious about one another and we've been thinking about trying to move in with each other."

Nicole told her everything and outlined Josh's plan to hire a nurse's aide to take care of her. As Nicole spoke, mom listened to every word with intentness – calculated intentness.

When Nicole was almost done talking, she then replied, "I'm surprised Josh hasn't told you already."

When Nicole said this, mom was looking at the floor – thinking.

But what was she thinking?

Then she perked up and said, "Actually he did already tell me. It was months ago. Yeah, he had been planning this for a while. Now I hate to be the bearer of bad news, but he got some other girl pregnant and he figured that by moving in with you that he would tell you at the right time and you would help him financially. I'm sorry if I caused any friction by telling you, but you're a really nice girl and I don't think Josh should take advantage of you like that."

Nicole put her hand up to her chest as if catching herself and with tears welling up in her eyes, she replied, "No, I think its best you did tell me. I needed to know."

"I'm so sorry, dear. So, what do you do from here?"

"Well, I guess it's over once and for all," Nicole sobbingly said wiping her eyes with her hands.

"There, there," mom soothingly said patting Nicole on her back.

"If you don't mind, I'd like to tell him it's over face to face. What time will he be home?"

"Oh, he'll be home around four."

"I can't believe him!"

Mom looked at Nicole with great satisfaction.

Mission accomplished.

Then that wry smile slid across her lips watching Nicole be angry at Josh and thinking just what she's done.

At 4:17 p.m. Josh came strolling in. He saw Nicole sitting there. He then exclaimed, "Hey honey," and he wanted to walk over and give her a kiss. But something stopped him. The look in her eyes is what stopped him cold in his tracks.

"Is everything alright, Nicole?" he concernedly asked.

Nicole then stood up and walked over to him. She then slapped him in the face hard and angrily replied, "Now everything is alright. Don't call me ever again."

Then she walked out the door.

I looked at mom who was looking at me and excitedly asked, "What the hell's going on?"

"Josh honey, listen. She never was any good for you. She came over to tell you that she found someone else."

"What!?"

I know it hurts honey, but believe me you'll get over her in time. Now can you be a sweetheart and go fix me a glass of freshly squeezed orange juice?"

"Yes, mother," I said gritting my teeth.

Then I made my way to the kitchen.

CHAPTER SEVENTEEN

For days I tried to reach Nicole, but she always ignored my calls.

What the hell was going on?!

We were really into one another for a while. I even thought we might have been falling in love with one another. The nights I layed in my bed thinking about Nicole and planning – planning a future with us walking down the aisle of holy matrimony and then someday even having kids.

But not now.

"I'm sorry I can't come to the phone right now. But if you leave me a brief message, I'll get back to you later is what I heard again before deciding to give up trying.

Then I heard mom calling me.

"Josh, Josh, come down honey. I want to talk to you."

I left my phone on the bed and went downstairs. When I got down there, there she was – waiting.

"Josh, come sit here close to me so I can speak to you."

I walked over and sat next to her.

"Josh," she began, "you know I only want what's best for you. I'm sorry I didn't tell you sooner, but I saw it all along. Now don't get mad at what I'm about to say, but Nicole is what you call a whore and I knew it a long time ago."

"Mom, how could you say such a thing?" I demanded.

"She just wanted to use you. Not saying she didn't have feelings for you, but she also had feelings for someone else – Marcus."

"What in the world are you talking about?"

"It's true, honey. One time she was over here and Marcus and Joseph were here also for dinner. Marcus went to the kitchen to put the rest of the food up. Then she said she had to go to the bathroom. But instead, she went to the kitchen where Marcus was and then approached him from behind and put her arms around his waist and kissed him on the neck. At first, he thought it was Ashley until he turned around and saw it was Nicole. He immediately flung her off of him and asked her what the hell she was doing. She responded by telling him that she knew he wanted her and that no one would find out. He then told her that he didn't see her that way and then asked her, how would Josh feel? She then remarked that you were just her boy toy and Marcus is who she wanted. He then told her that he would let this one slide, but don't break Josh's heart and do this ever again. So you see, Josh, I knew this would all come about this with her because that's the kind of girl she is. I just hoped that you would see what she was for yourself before it came to this. I would've told you earlier, but I couldn't because I didn't have the nerve and I didn't want to break your heart."

"I guess I found out the hard way. And to think, we were looking at trying to move in with each other."

I'm just glad it's over.

It's good to know that my mom loves me enough to let me know what she tried with my oldest brother and stopping me from making the mistake of moving in with that conniving whore.

I went for a walk to clear my head and my conscience of Nicole. I never wanted to see her again. And to think, I was so in love with her. I thought she was perfect for me.

Life is so unfair.

Now I wondered to myself, "Will I ever find love again?"

But this pain that I felt now made me bitter and wanting to reject any woman who came along with any interest in me.

Feeling upset and drained, I sat down on a bench. It was then that two little girls came running past me merrily laughing and playing. I then thought to myself, "When was the last time I was that happy?"

I can't remember.

It was then and there that I longed for comfort; for the company of someone who could relate to what I was going through. I pulled my phone out and decided to call dad.

After a few rings, he answered, "Hello."

"Hey dad."

"Oh hey, Josh. How ya doin'?"

"Terrible."

"Oh whatever it is can't be that bad. What's wrong?"

"My girlfriend dumped me. And get this, the whole time she had eyes for Marcus. She even made a move on him."

"Wow, I gotta say I didn't expect to hear anything like that. But the best part is that life goes on. There's plenty of other girls out there. Forget about her and move on."

"I don't know if I can. She was the love of my life. I don't think I'll ever love another girl."

"Look, you're being too hard on yourself. You're going about this the wrong way."

There was silence for about five to ten seconds.

Then Jacob piped up, "Listen, how about we discuss this over a nice cup of coffee."

"Sounds good, dad."

"Where are you?"

"I'm at Cobblestone Park."

"Alright, I'll be there in about ten minutes. We can go to 'Second Best Coffee' and sit down and talk."

"O.K."

"Alright, I'll see you in a little bit."

"O.K., bye."

"Bye."

Meanwhile, back at home, mom, Marcus, and Joseph are all there gathered in the living room. Suddenly a knock at the door. Joseph opened it to see Nicole standing there.

"Hey Joseph," she replied. "I didn't come to stay or talk. I just wanted to tell Josh to take my number out of his phone so that he'll never call me again."

Then the wheels got to turning in mom's mind.

"Nicole," she began, "I know you're very upset and hurt about Josh."

"Yes, I certainly am," she responded starting to get a little watery-eyed just thinking about it.

"Are you upset enough to do anything about it?" mom replied. "You know, they say what goes around comes around."

"Well what did you have in mind?" Nicole confusingly asked.

"Come on in and we'll discuss this."

Nicole then stepped in and Joseph closed the door behind her.

Exactly twelve minutes after I talked to dad on the phone, he came pulling up in his truck.

"Hey Josh," he replied.

"Hey dad."

"Hop in."

I did and then we were headed for 'Second Best Coffee.'

When we got there, we parked, then got out, and went in. The first thing we did, as if on instinct, was to inhale deeply the aroma of freshly brewed coffee.

Then Jacob replied, "Nothing like that scent to really get your day going."

Then we approached the counter.

I began to take in the sights of this place. The different decorations and photographs of famous people made it look magnificent.

"Wow," I thought.

I was so entranced with the layout and just on the way it appeared, I didn't even notice dad talking to me until he nudged me.

"Josh, Josh," he exclaimed, "he asked you what you would like. I already ordered mine."

"Oh, I'll just have a latte," I announced snapping back to reality. It wasn't really what I wanted, but I was caught off guard and kind-of rushed to order, so I just said anything.

"What'd you order?" I asked.

"I got a cappuccino."

When the man behind the counter told us the total, I pulled my wallet out and began to phish for a twenty dollar bill only to look up and see dad handing him a twenty. The man then rung it up and gave dad his change. He then went to prepare our order. After we got our beverages, dad motioned towards an empty table near the back. The one thing I noticed was that there were lots of people there who appeared to be couples. It got me to thinking of Nicole.

Why hadn't I taken her here before?

Then dad and I sat down.

"So do you want to tell me what's really wrong? I sense that something else is bothering you besides being dumped by your girlfriend."

"Yes, something else is wrong, but the weird thing is I can't place it."

"Yeah, that is weird," he responded. But there was something about his look. It was the exact same look he had the night he left. It was like he knew some things that he was intentionally holding back.

I decided to ask him something that had been on my mind for years.

"Dad, what happened the night you left? What could have been so horrible to make you leave your entire family in one night?"

He obviously didn't want to answer this question as I could see the pain in his eyes fighting for a response to my inquiry. But I had already laid it out and like it or not, we weren't going anywhere until I got my answer and he knew it.

Finally the best answer he could give me was, "You'll find out when the time is right."

"What does that mean?"

Dad, sensing that I was getting persistent for an answer, suddenly stood up and began fumbling. "I have to go. I'm sorry, but I must be getting on now."

"Dad, wait."

But he didn't wait. He turned around and began walking and soon enough he was out the door.

CHAPTER EIGHTEEN

I tried to act cheerful around mom and around Joseph and Marcus when they would come to visit. But there was no faking it, I was depressed. I thought to myself, "How dare she cheat on me and make a move on my older brother."

I told myself, "It's a very good thing that she is gone."

The truth was I missed her dearly.

As the days went on, I tried to focus on anything but Nicole. It was hard, but I was determined to manage. At work, I tried to get a new attitude and I thought that if I worked harder, that it would make me forget about all of this.

I was wrong.

Next, I tried to adopt exercising to help me cope. I would spend my extra time lifting weights, doing push-ups, sit-ups, and crunches.

It was useless.

I even tried meditating. I would sit on the floor in my room with my legs crossed and eyes closed trying to focus and channel my energy on peaceful things.

But to no avail.

I would always go back to the look on her face when she saw me that day and then the dreaded slap.

Then one day I was sitting on my bed when I picked up my notebook off of the dresser. I began thumbing through it.

It was the first draft to "Forbidden Truth" that I had written.

Then it hit me.

Why not write another book?

Yeah, that's it. That'll definitely take my mind off of her. I'll write a science-fiction book.

And I figured no time like the present to get started. So I pulled out a fresh notebook and an ink pen and began: "The Chronicles of the Sons of Darkness."

I wrote and wrote and before long I had my introduction finished. I found this to be very relaxing and stress-free. So the next day I wrote more, then the next day more and so forth, and actually found that by focusing on my writing, the less I thought about Nicole. So every chance I got, I would write. I found myself working on it so much that in little time I was almost done.

Just like with the first book, I decided to have my copy delivered to the house and let mom see it so that she would be surprised. But something told me this was a bad idea.

But I don't know what.

Finally, the book was done and the same company that published "Forbidden Truth" published this one also.

Then one day the doorbell rang and it was the UPS man with a package for me.

"Josh, what is that?" mom groaned half-awake and half-sleep.

I opened the package and there I stood with my second published book in hand.

"Mom look."

"What is that, Josh?"

"It's another book I wrote. I didn't tell you about it till now because I wanted you to be surprised."

She sprung up and with the widest eyes replied, "You did what?"

Then she put her hand to her mouth in amazement. Actually, it was more like horror than amazement.

Then her eyes began to squint as she looked from the book to me and from me to the book.

Then I exclaimed, "Careful mom, you'll hurt yourself."

She then put her hand to her head and as she layed back down and responded, "Oh my, the pain, the pain."

"Mom, aren't you surprised?"

"Oh yes, honey. I'm more than surprised."

"I can tell."

CHAPTER NINETEEN

"Oh darn. I can't find it anywhere."

"Find what, Josh? What are you looking for?" mom inquired.

"My I.D. The last place I remember putting it was in my wallet as usual."

It had been missing for months now.

"Oh, you'll find it. Just don't worry about it. Come talk to me about your book."

I went over and sat down and told her what the book was about. Half-way through my talking, there came a knock at the door.

"Come in," mom replied.

In stepped Joseph and Marcus.

"Oh hey, boys. It's good seeing you," mom joyfully responded.

"It's good seeing you too," Joseph replied as he and Marcus made their way over to the couch to hug mom.

"Oh hey, Josh," Joseph said as he turned his attention to me.

"Hey Joseph and Marcus," I exclaimed as I stood there looking at the two of them.

"If you don't mind, I think I'll go lay down for a little bit. It's probably just something I ate," I said rubbing my stomach.

Then I went upstairs.

There was actually nothing wrong with my stomach. I just wanted to get away. I didn't feel right being in the same room with all of them. Instead of going to my room, I decided to go to the attic.

When I got there, I opened the door and walked in. I walked over and sat in the cushion chair. After a few minutes of sitting there, I stood up and then was headed out. As I made my way to the door, I heard CREAK. I stopped and walked back on the spot where I heard it and then I heard it again – CREAK. I thought, "That's odd. I didn't know we had any loose floor boards."

But when I looked at the board I was stepping on, I could see it was very loose. So I knelt down to examine it and when I pulled it just a little, the whole board came up. There were little slips of paper – lots of them. I picked one of them up and looked at it. It was a cashed pay stub for $19,180.

"What the hell?"

I picked another one up. It read $21,240. Then I picked up another and another. They were all pay stubs.

Then I remembered the incident just last week with mom. I was in the living room with her when my publishing company called. I put them on speaker phone. Before they could say two words, mom blurted out, "Josh, hang up. They're a scam artist. They just want your money. Then the person over the phone replied, "Josh, great news. Do you have a moment?"

Mom then exclaimed, "No Josh, they just want money. I had someone do research on them and they're not a legitimate company."

"But Mr. McClure, if I could just have one moment of your time..."

"Josh, hang up now. You know I would never lead you wrong. I would never lie to you. I'm your mother for God's sakes!"

"Please don't call me ever again," I calmly said, then hung up.

As I stood there with those paid stubs in my hand, it hit me.

My I.D. didn't come up missing, Joseph stole it because as my twin brother he can pass for me and easily have cashed my checks for my royalties from my books. My publishing company called me to tell me my books were selling and mom tricked me in to telling them to never calling me again and hanging up on them before they could tell me the good news.

I went downstairs to confront them.

When I got down there, I saw them all together and I announced, "What the hell is going on?"

"What do you mean?" Joseph asked.

"You know exactly what I mean. You've stolen my I.D. and have been cashing my checks for my royalties."

"Josh, what are you talking about?"

"No boys," mom chimed in. "The charade is up. Yes Josh, Joseph has been cashing your checks. So what of it? I think it's time we set the record straight right now. I never really loved you. I only cared about Joseph and Marcus. Your whole life has been a lie. Do you really want to know why your father left when you were young? Well that night in the room, I told him how I wanted you to be miserable all of your life and I would do anything to make sure that happened. He then wanted to take custody of you, but I had very powerful lawyer friends so rather than fight a battle in court he knew he would lose, he just decided to leave because he couldn't bear to watch it happen. You know what else, Josh, the poem that you wrote when you were younger. Yes, I did turn it in and win that $500. And then there's this so-called accident I had. I have news for you, she said standing up, I faked the whole thing. I just wanted to hold you back from getting your own place and being independent like your brothers because I didn't want you being happy."

"Enough is enough," I thought.

Joseph was sitting on the couch. I hurriedly walked over to him and placed my hands on his chin and top of his head and snapped his neck. In one instant, he was dead.

Then Marcus ran to me and screamed, "You shouldn't have done that! You're dead!"

He then swung with a right hook. I ducked and then came up with an upper-cut to the stomach. I then grabbed him by the head and snapped his neck too.

He was dead.

Then I turned my sights toward mom. As I advanced towards her closer and closer, she screamed, "No, Josh don't! I'm your mother."

Then I reached out and grabbed her by the head and snapped her neck and she was dead too.

Then I walked over and sat on the floor and looked at the carnage I had created. I pulled out my cell phone and called dad and told him what just took place. I could hear dad crying as he replied, "You know, I prayed every day that you would get out of there so you could get your own life and be away from them. But I can't say that I didn't see this day coming."

"What do I do now?"

"Don't try to run and avoid the police. Just turn yourself in."

Then I hung up on daddy and called the police and told them what I had done.

EPILOGUE

I am now on death row waiting to die. My books began to sell more and more and even became nationwide bestsellers. Soon they were made into movies. I then wrote a book from prison entitled "The Silent Deception" that was also made into a movie.

My dad visits me often with prayer and words of encouragement. I am now sitting in my cell with my hands cuffed staring into nothingness.

"Joshua Eugene McClure," the guard said as he unlocked the cell.

"Yes, that's me," I said standing up and walking out of the cell.

"Seems like a wonderful day – for the electric chair," the guard replied.

Jacob and Nicole both are at the execution. As they strap Joshua into the chair, he screams out, "They had it coming! I'm the victim here!"

Finally they had him strapped in securely. Oh how it pained Jacob to see his baby boy like this. Then they flipped the switch. And just like that, it was done.

Once it was over, Jacob saw Nicole and approaches her and introduces himself as Joshua's father. Nicole then says that she was Joshua's ex-girlfriend. Jacob then replies, "I have no idea why you wanted to hurt Joshua and break his heart. He told me that he was nothing but good to you." Then Nicole put a smirk on her face and replied, "I've got news for you. I'm pregnant with Joshua's baby and I'm keeping it.

SUMMARY

Joshua McClure was born into this world unsure. He was unsure about the love that he was so certain his family had for him. As he is growing up, he begins to question more and more the truth behind the dark secrets looming in his family. When his mom takes ill and he had to care for her later in life, the questions arise like never before. Then one day when his family is together and he is in the attic, he finds out a shocking secret. This secret climaxes the story with an ending that will leave you breathless.

www.ingramcontent.com/pod-product-compliance
Lightning Source LLC
LaVergne TN
LVHW032005070526
838202LV00058B/6307